A lost cause.

I turned around all right, but once I turned around, I found myself . . . well, turned around, you might say, and it's a well known fact that you can't backtrack if you lost the track and don't know which way is back.

All at once I found myself basically lost. I had lost the scent, the trail, my sense of direction, my sense of well being, my courage, my confidence, my curiosity, and my devotion to duty. But most of all, I had lost all desire to be where I was.

Why didn't I leave the forest? There's a very simple explanation for that. A guy can't leave what he doesn't like unless he knows where to go to find something better. And I didn't.

Lost in the
Dark Unchanted Forest

Lost in the
Dark Unchanted Forest

John R. Erickson

Illustrations by Gerald L. Holmes

Puffin Books

PUFFIN BOOKS
Published by the Penguin Group
Penguin Putnam Books for Young Readers,
345 Hudson Street, New York, New York 10014, U.S.A.
Penguin Books Ltd,
27 Wrights Lane, London W8 5TZ, England
Penguin Books Australia Ltd,
Ringwood, Victoria, Australia
Penguin Books Canada Ltd,
10 Alcorn Avenue, Toronto, Ontario, Canada M4V 3B2
Penguin Books (N.Z.) Ltd,
182-190 Wairau Road, Auckland 10, New Zealand
Penguin Books Ltd, Registered Offices:
Harmondsworth, Middlesex, England

First published in the United States of America by
Maverick Books, Gulf Publishing Company, 1988

Published by Puffin Books, a member of
Penguin Putnam Books for Young Readers, 1999

7 9 10 8 6

Hank the Cowdog® is a registered trademark of John R. Erickson.

LIBRARY OF CONGRESS CATALOGING-IN-PUBLICATION DATA
Erickson, John R.
Lost in the dark unchanted forest / John R. Erickson ;
illustrations by Gerald L. Holmes.
p. cm.
Originally published in series: Hank the Cowdog ; 11.
Summary: Fearless Hank the Cowdog, Head of Ranch Security, enters the
"dark unchanted forest" to rescue his master's son from Sinister the bobcat.
ISBN 0-14-130387-5 (pbk.)
[1. Dogs—Fiction. 2. West (U.S.)—Fiction. 3. Humorous stories.
4. Mystery and detective stories.] I. Holmes, Gerald L., ill. II. Title.
III. Series: Erickson, John R. Hank the Cowdog ; 11.
PZ7.E72556Lo 1999 [Fic]—dc21 98-41815 CIP AC

Printed in the United States of America

CONTENTS

CHAPTER ONE

Mauled by a Gigantic Sniveling Cat

It's me again, Hank the Cowdog. It was your typical spring day, nothing out of the ordinary: calm, bright, a little on the warmish side, the air full of cotton from the cottonwood trees.

We were up around the machine shed, as I recall, basking in the sun, whiling away the afternoon, and waiting for darkness to fall, at which time we would begin our night patrol. Since Loper and Sally May had left the ranch the day before on a mysterious trip to a place called "Hospital," I had made the decision to double up on night patrol.

Drover was over by the water well, engaged in

1

a meaningless conversation with J. T. Cluck, the head rooster. Suddenly he called.

"Hank, come here and look at this thing and tell us what you think it is."

I responded to the call and studied the object before him. "That's a rooster."

"No, I mean this down here." He pointed his nose to the ground.

"Oh." I looked down, sniffed it out, and studied the clues. "That's dirt, Drover, just common ordinary dirt."

"Yeah, I know, but is that some kind of print or track in the dirt?"

"Oh." I ran a more thorough search this time, and that's when I found the mysterious track. I raised up my head—slowly, so as not to alarm anyone—and glanced over both shoulders to see if we were being watched. "Where did you find this track?"

"Well, it was right there in the dirt."

"That checks out. Who knows about it?"

"Just me and J.T., I guess."

"Question: Has anyone or anything passed by here in the last hour?"

"Well, just me and J.T. and a fly . . . a big, noisy fly."

"And therefore you think the fly left this track, is that what you're saying? Nice try, Drover. I saw the alleged fly and I know he was big, but not big enough to leave tracks like this. I don't want to alarm anyone, but I should point out that this is one of the biggest tracks I've ever seen."

"Yeah, I know. That's just what J.T. said when he found it. He thought maybe it was a bobcat track."

I gave the runt a withering glare. "Number One, J.T. didn't find this track. I did."

"Now just a darn minute!" said J.T.

3

I snapped at him, relieved him of a few feathers, and sent him on his way. The last thing I needed was a noisy chicken around to disrupt my investigation—especially one that would try to hog some of the credit for my careful work.

I turned back to Drover. "Number Two, you should disregard anything J.T. might have said about this track, because chickens don't know beans about tracks. Number Three, we haven't seen a bobcat on this ranch in years. Number Four, this track was made by an exceptionally large boar coon.

"Number Five, I'm betting he's still hiding on the ranch; and Number Six, our primary mission on tonight's patrol will be to search him out and throw him off the place before he gets into some serious mischief."

"You mean . . ."

"Exactly. Prepare for combat, Drover. Catch all the sleep you can between now and dark. I have a feeling we'll need it."

He sniffed at the track. "It sure doesn't look like a coon track to me."

"Stick with what you do best, son. Sleep. I'll get you up at 2100 hours."

At precisely 2100 hours I awakened Drover and we began what turned out to be one of the most dangerous patrols of my career. It began in a fairly routine manner, with us checking out the saddle shed, the medicine shed, the sick pen, the front lot, and the side lot.

Nothing. And yet . . .

Maybe I have a sick sense, a sixth sense, that is, about these things, a still small voice that warns me when something isn't right. It was trying to warn me when I headed for the feed barn.

We stopped in front of the door and I dropped my voice to a whisper. "Drover, my hunch tells me that our friend the coon is in the feed barn. Chances are that he has busted into a sack of horse feed and he's eating the corn and molasses out of it. I'll go in first."

"I hear that."

"We'll hold you in reserve just outside the door. If things get bad, I may have to call you in. Come on, let's move out."

I slipped up to the door. This is the one that's warped at the bottom, you might recall, which allowed me to wiggle the top half of my body inside without committing the bottom half. Once in that position, I did a scan and . . .

I wiggled outside again, leaned my back against the side of the shed, and laughed. I couldn't help it. It was just too good to be true.

Drover watched me with a puzzled expression. "What's so funny?"

"You won't believe this. We have just been handed the best ornery prank of the year. You know who that is in there? Not a coon, Drover, but Pete the Barncat!"

"Pete? Are you sure?"

"He must be looking for mice, see. He's got his front-end on the ground and his hind-end up in the air and his head between two bales of hay. He thinks he's all alone in the world, and when I go crashing in there and jump right in the middle of him, he'll think he's been attacked by a big boar coon!"

"Sounds pretty good . . . if it is Pete."

"Of course it's Pete. Don't you think I know the scent of a cat?"

"Yeah, but . . ."

"The place reeks of cat. Why, he couldn't smell any cattier if he'd been living in the wild for the last six months."

"Hank?"

"Hush. The time has come. Stand by for a barrel of laughs, because I'm fixing to let the cat out of the bag."

"Yeah, but which cat?"

I slipped through the door again, all the way

this time. A few arrows of moonlight were coming through the cracks in the roof, just enough so that I could make a visual confirmation of my original nosatory data. Everything checked out. We had us a cat cornered, fellers, and the fun was about to begin.

I took a big gulp of air, leaped through the air, and yelled, "Watch out for the boar coon, Pete!"

I had reached the apex of my dive and had

begun my downward arc when I noticed . . . hmmm, Pete's tail had been shortened. And come to think of it, his coat had changed colors—white with dark spots—and . . . by George, he looked bigger than I . . . real big, almost the size of a . . . HUH?

Holy smokes, do you realize how big and tough bobcats are? They're terrible! I wouldn't jump on a bobcat for all the bones in Texas, and yet . . .

I tried to make some mid-course corrections, began moving my front feet in a dog paddle mode, but it was too late. I straddled him, fellers, landed right in the middle of his back.

You think a bobcat can't buck? Think again. He throwed an arch in his back and blew me right out of my rigging. I went straight up in the air, hit my head on a ceiling joist, and started back down. But before I hit the ground, this giant maniac of a cat slapped me across the mouth with a paw that was about the size of a T-bone steak.

That sent me flying in a different direction, south this time, until I came to the south wall, and at that point I came to a sudden stop and dropped in a heap on the floor.

I was seeing stars and checkers and little pink elephants with umbrellas, but that didn't keep me from getting a real good look at the monster cat: big, mean, ugly, ferocious. Your ordinary bob-cat is about two or three times the size of your ordinary barncat. This guy was two or three times the size of your ordinary *bobcat*.

I'd seen him before, at a distance. His name was Sinister the Bobcat. He was a cold-blooded professional killer with a rap sheet as long as your leg, and I had definitely made a big mistake.

"Drover, I don't want to alarm you, but at this moment I am trapped in the feed barn with a gigantic bobcat."

"Oh my gosh! Then J.T. was right about the tracks!"

"I wouldn't put it exactly that way, but the point is that our main column is surrounded. It's time to bring up the reserves." I heard the swish of something moving through the air at a high rate of speed, then silence. "Drover? Drover!"

The runt had abandoned me. Sinister took a step in my direction, his long white teeth glowing in the darkness.

"Hi there, you're Sinister the Bobcat, I believe. We haven't met, but I . . . you probably won't believe this, but I came in here looking for a cousin of yours, Pete the . . . yes sir, old Pete and I have been friends for . . . obviously you're not Pete and I probably ought to be . . ."

9

He took another step towards me, and I could tell at a glance that he didn't want to talk about his kinfolks.

"Now Sinister, I've always figgered that there's a middle ground between surrender and annihilation, and if you'd care to discuss . . . "

Sinister wasn't a talker. I knew that the instant he knocked me back up into the rafters. Coming down, I tried to latch onto one of the ceiling joists but couldn't quite hang on. I headed for the floor again, but never reached it because Sinister caught me under the chin with a roundhouse right that sent me flying south again, only this one knocked me through the window, thank goodness.

There was an explosion of glass and I woke up, draped over one of the lower branches of an elm tree. I climbed out of the tree and tested my wobbly legs. I still had all four of 'em.

I glanced through the busted window and saw Sinister inside the feed barn, turning over bales of hay and looking for mice. He didn't even look tired, which kind of annoyed me.

"Sinister, you got lucky this time, but next time . . ."

He made a move in my direction and I sold out, didn't slow down until I limped up to the gas tanks. I found Drover hiding beneath his gunny-sack bed.

"Drover, you'll be interested in knowing that, even without your help, I just suffered an incredible beating."

He stuck his nose out the west side. "Well, I didn't think it would help for both of us to get beat up."

"That's very noble of you, son, and I promise I won't forget this."

"Thanks, Hank."

"And the next time you need someone to come to your rescue, call a cat."

I flopped down on my gunnysack. Everything hurt, especially my pride. For a dog, there is nothing to compare with the humilification of being pounded by a sniveling cat—even a big sniveling cat.

I cancelled night patrol and went to sleep.

CHAPTER TWO

The Giant Baldheaded Lizard

I awoke the next morning at the crack of noon. What woke me was the sound of a car coming down the road towards the house.

I leaped to my feet and . . . oh mercy! . . . was suddenly reminded that only hours before I had been mauled by a bobcat. I limped and hobbled out to challenge the trespassers and . . . oh, it was Loper and Sally May, back from their trip to Hospital, wherever that was.

When I realized that we had a friendly car coming onto the ranch, I shifted out of Serious Barking Mode and limped out to greet them.

Loper got out and rubbed me on the head. "You've got ticks," he said, and went around to the other side of the car.

He opened the door and helped Sally May out. She was carrying something in her arms, something wrapped up in a pink blanket.

Drover had joined me by then and he saw it too. "What's that?"

"Groceries, what do you think?"

"I thought groceries came in a brown sack."

"Most of the time they do, Drover, but now and then they wrap them up in pink blankets."

"Oh."

Sally May was smiling, beaming. I'd never seen her in such a good humor. Those must have been pretty good groceries. I figgered this might be a good time to mend a few fences, so to speak, with the lady of the house, so I went around to the other side of the car.

"Oh look, Molly, there's old Hank, and there's little Drover."

That was odd. She seemed to be speaking to the groceries. But that was okay because she was still smiling. As long as Sally May's smiling and not throwing rocks, I don't care what she talks to.

"Dogs," she said, "I've brought home a special surprise for you."

I glanced at Drover. "You see? She went to the grocery store and got us some nice juicy bones."

"Oh good! Boy, do I like bones!"

13

"But I get first dibs, son. Don't forget who's in charge here."

Sally May uncovered the top part of the bundle and bent down so that we could...

When I saw what was inside that blanket, fellers, the hair shot up on my back and my throat began making a sound that was something between a growl and a gurgle.

Holy smokes! *Sally May had brought home a giant lizard from the grocery store!*

Well, you know me. When confronted with something new and ugly and terrible, I don't just stand there looking foolish. *I bark.*

Yes indeed, I barked. I had no idea why Sally May had brought that thing home or what she planned to do with it, but I staked out my territory and barked up a storm. And just in case the lizard attacked, I also retreated a few steps.

You know what Sally May and Loper did? They started *laughing.* Beat anything I ever saw. I mean, they had just brought a strange and possibly dangerous animal onto the ranch, and then...

Sally May gave me another look at the thing's head, which was unnecessary because I'd already seen all I needed to see. "Hank, don't be silly. It's just a baby."

"It's just a baby," Drover said.

I glared at the runt. "I seem to be hearing an echo."

"No, that was me. I said . . ."

"I heard what you said and I heard what she said, and you don't need to repeat everything you hear. I'm not deaf and that's no baby. It's the first full-grown Giant Baldheaded Lizard I've ever seen on this ranch."

"But Hank, it's not a lizard. It's Sally May's new baby."

HUH?

15

I studied the creature again: two eyes, two ears, one mouth, one nose, red skin, and wrinkles, and inside the blanket, two arms, two legs, and a nightgown.

Hmmmmm. The pieces of the puzzle were beginning . . . okay, maybe it wasn't a . . . let's put it this way: that was a very strange looking baby, and any dog who was in charge of Ranch Security would have . . .

"All right, Drover, I think I've got this thing puzzled out. Sally May went to the town of Hospital and bought herself a baby at the grocery store. Instead of putting it in a brown paper sack, as they usually do, they wrapped it up in a pink blanket, and what we have here before us now is NOT a lizard."

"Yeah, I know."

"It's a human baby child."

"That's what I said."

"And we can only hope that the poor little thing gets more attractive with time, because it certainly looks like a Giant Baldheaded Lizard to me."

"I think she's kind of cute."

"Anyone with a face like yours would think that a lizard was cute."

Sally May bent down and held the thing, uh,

the baby up where I could see it, her, whatever it was. "Hank, this is Molly. And Molly, this is Hank. Hank, I want you to take good care of little Miss Molly. She's a real treasure."

I eased my nose towards the face and sniffed it several times. Okay, what we had here was a human baby child, a girl named Molly. She belonged to Sally May and Loper, and right then and there I took an oath to protect and defend her against monsters, snakes, and other crawling things. Even bobcats.

And to seal the oath, I licked her on the face. For some reason, the little creature let out a squall.

Sally May must not have understood the importance of this gesture or the seriousness of the occasion, for she jerked the baby back and shrieked at me.

"DON'T LICK MY BABY, YOU MORON!" Then Loper came thundering up. "Hank, for crying out loud, don't lick the baby!"

I tucked my tail between my legs and retreated a few steps, and then Drover, the little goof, said, "You better not lick the baby."

I glared at him. "Drover, you needn't repeat the obvious."

"Yeah, but you licked her on the face with your tongue and that's not nice."

"Would it have been nicer if I'd licked her on the foot with my ear?"

He rolled his eyes. "Well, I don't know about that."

"The answer is no, it wouldn't have been nicer. It would have been impossible. Her foot was covered up and my ears don't lick. I did what I could do with what I had, and no dog could have done more than that."

"Yeah, but you could have done less."

"Exactly my point. And now we come to the final summation of everything I've been saying."

"Oh good. What is it?"

"Shut your little trap."

"Oh, well that sure sums it up."

Sally May carried her baby into the house and Loper followed with a bunch of suitcases and bags. They left Little Alfred, who was four years old, out in the yard. He was wearing a pair of striped overalls and had his hands stuck in the pockets.

Also, I noticed that his lower lip was sticking out. He didn't look very happy, seemed to me, and I went over to cheer him up. He kicked a rock and looked at me.

"I don't wike that baby. I want to take her back to the hospito."

Well, I had a little talk with the boy and tried to explain things to him. Me and Alfred were special pals, see. I'd helped raise the boy and we'd always been able to talk things over.

"Son," I said, "I know that your little sister ain't very pretty right now, and she makes a lot of noise, but she'll grow out of it and one of these days you'll be proud to have her on the place."

"No I won't. You don't care about me and you're not my fwiend anymore and I don't wike you either. And I'm going to hit you."

I wagged my tail and tried to . . .

Would you believe it? The little snot slapped me right across the nose! If anybody else had done that, fellers, I would have removed his arm and half a leg. But you might recall that, many years before, I had taken the Cowdog Oath and sworn never to bite a child—even one that deserved it.

So I didn't bite him. And he hit me again. And then he grabbed my tail and started dragging me around the yard. I had seen him do this to Pete the Barncat on several occasions and had, well, enjoyed it, you might say.

But that had been a different deal entirely. When he'd been dragging Pete around, that had been good wholesome entertainment because, after all, what else is a cat good for? But this time, with me on the short end of the stick, so to speak, *it hurt*.

Oh, it did hurt! My tail is a very sensitive and expressive communication device, and it was never intended to be pecked by chickens, stepped on by cowboys, or pulled by bratty little boys. I mean, Alfred was putting my Cowdog Oath to the test, and if I'd had just a smidgen less of iron discipline . . .

I squalled. I cried. I moaned. Heck, a guy has to do something to protect himself from these little monsters.

It was my good fortune that Sally May had good ears. She came flying out the back door, sized up the situation with one sweep of her eyes, and marched over to Little Alfred.

"Alfred, what on earth are you doing?"

He gave her a nasty little grin. "I'm pwaying wiff Hank."

"You're *hurting* Hank. Hank doesn't like for you to pull his tail. Now let go, right now!"

The boy let go of my tail. "I don't wike Hank. He's a dummy."

Oh yeah? Well, I could have come up with a few choice names for him, too.

Sally May took him by the shoulders and gave

20

him a shake. "If you can't be nice to Hank, you can't play with him. You play quietly with your trucks while we put Molly down for a nap."

Alfred glared up at her and stuck out his lip. "I don't wike Mah-wee either!"

"Hush now. Mommy will be right out to play with you."

She went back into the house. When she was out of hearing range, Alfred made a spitting sound with his lips. Then he made another grab for me, but this time he was half a step too slow. I went sprinting out of the yard and picked up Drover at the gate.

"Come on, Drover, let's get out of here."

I didn't know what had come over the boy and I didn't care to find out. I figgered it was time to let Little Alfred stew in his own tomatoes.

CHAPTER THREE

Swimming
Lessons for Pete

We went sprinting up the hill, trotted past the chicken house, scattered the chickens, and went to the machine shed.

I've always enjoyed scattering chickens. Even on days when I'm in a bad mood and nothing seems to be going right, I can run through a bunch of chickens and, I don't know, it just seems to give new meaning to my life.

I was still feeling sore from my beating the previous night, and also hungry, so I spent several minutes crunching Co-op dog food from the overturned Ford hubcap which serves as our bowl.

Many times I've wondered how much it would cost the ranch to buy us a real bowl, instead of a

nasty hubcap that retains the taste of axle grease. Yes, I know. Grass is short and cattle prices are down, but I also know that the cowboys on this outfit eat out of plates and bowls, not hubcaps.

It's funny to me that there always seems to be enough grass and enough cattle market to buy plates for *them,* but you mention buying anything decent for the Head of Ranch Security, and suddenly we're in the midst of a drought and a plague and a depression!

I mean, the cattle market has fallen off the edge of the world and there ain't a sprig of grass left in the pastures and everybody's going around in rags and their toes are poking out of the holes in their boots and they're having to boil tree bark to feed the children.

It makes a guy think that the people in charge don't realize just how important their dogs are to the overall . . . oh well.

I ate dog food out of the hubcap and tried not to think of all the injustices in the world. Too much brooding can ruin your digestion, and life without digestion is . . . something. Unbearable. Full of burps. Hard to bear.

Yes, we crunched our dog food: hard, dry, yellowish kernels that come in a fifty pound sack. Sometimes I wonder what kind of stuff they put into those kernels, and other times I'd just as soon not know.

I noticed that Drover was making a lot of noise. "Do you suppose you could be a little quieter in chewing your food?"

"Well, I don't know, Hank. It's pretty hard."

"Of course it is. It's always harder to eat with manners than to eat with the wild abandon of a hog, but who wants to sound like a hog?"

"Not me."

"Hogs make no pretense at being civilized, Drover. They crunch and smack and grunt, and nobody cares because they're only hogs who eat like pigs."

"That makes sense."

"But we're not hogs, Drover. We aspire to something higher and better. We try to bring a certain air of dignity to the ritual of eating. The act of imposing dignity on the chaos of experience is called *civilization,* and protecting civilization has always been hard."

"Yeah, but I meant the kernels were hard."

"Oh."

"Hard to chew." He crunched a kernel.

"Yes, I see what you . . ." I crunched a kernel, "mean. They are hard, aren't they? In fact, they hurt my teeth."

"Yeah, and they hurt my gums."

"You shouldn't be chewing gum while you eat, Drover. Not only do you run the risk of swallowing it and gumming up your entrails, but it's also in very poor taste."

"Yeah, it tastes kind of like sawdust to me."

"Exactly. But taste and manners are like grease in the ball bearings of experience. Without the grease, we would have nothing but friction and disharmony."

"You reckon they add a little grease to improve the taste?"

"There's no explaining taste, Drover. Some dogs have it and some don't. Those of us who do, and I include myself in that group, have the added burden of defending it against the endless assaults of the mindless rubble."

"Yeah, and the chickens."

At that very moment, a chicken came up to our dog bowl and appeared to be thinking of pecking into our food. I lowered my head, lifted my lips, exposed my teeth, and snarled.

"Get away from our food, you feather merchant!"

She squawked and ran, and we went back to our eating. Drover wore a big grin on his face as he smacked and crunched.

"Boy, we're pretty good at defending our taste, even if it tastes like sawdust."

"Someone has to do it, Drover, and it might as well be us."

All at once we heard a commotion coming from somewhere down below. My ears, which are very sensitive and operate pretty muchly independent of the rest of my body, picked up the sound, and within seconds had passed the information along to Data Control.

There the sound was analyzed, broken down into vectors and parameters, and given a specific location. The mental printout which appeared behind my eyes contained this brief message: "DISTRESSED CAT NEAR SEPTIC TANK."

I went on eating. We respond to most distress calls at once, but a cat in distress can always wait until we finish our meal.

But then I heard the back door slam. I paused, switched my ears from automatic to manual, lifted them a half-inch, and opened the exterior flaps to increase their sound gathering capacity.

Footsteps on the sidewalk. The squeak of the yard gate. The snap of the gate latch. Footsteps on gravel. Sally May's voice.

"Alfred? Alfred? Where did you go?"

More footsteps on the gravel, moving down the hill towards the gas tanks. "REEEEEEEER!" That was the cat again, no problem there. Ah ha!

A splashing sound. A child laughing. Then Sally May again.

"Alfred! What on earth?"

I sighed and stood up. "Swallow your food, Drover, we've got a Code Three down at the septic tank."

Drover had a mouthful. "Acktock cwqbhd sclcke bdkdkejald."

"I can't understand you. Your mouth is full."

"Cvkwlcled ckwoeidke bjeildhck flwe."

"Swallow, clear your moth . . . your mouth, that is, and try it again."

He chewed and swallowed hard. "I said, my mouth is full."

"No, it's clear now. I'm getting a good copy on you."

"I know, I just swallered what it was full of."

"I know you just swallered it. That's what I told you to do, that's what you did, so what's the problem?"

"I don't know. My mouth was full and I couldn't talk and that's what I was trying to tell you."

"You tried to tell me but your mouth was full and you weren't able to communicate your message, is that correct?"

"Yeah, that's exactly what happened."

"So . . . what is the point of this discussion?"

"I don't know. Don't run around when your mouth's full or you might choke . . . I guess."

I glared at the runt. "You're taking the time to tell me *that* when we've got a Code Three down at the septic tank?"

"I was just minding my own business and trying to eat and . . ."

"Drover, sometimes I think . . . never mind. We've got a job to do. Stay behind me and let's move out!"

We went streaking away from the machine shed, down the hill, past the gas tanks, and towards the overflow of the septic tank. There the scene unfolded before us.

Little Alfred had just pitched the cat into the overflow of the septic tank. The cat appeared to be waterlogged and angry. His ears were flattened against his head and water dripped off his chin. He bounded through the shallow water until he reached dry land, where he stood dripping water and glaring daggers at anyone who cared to look at his sorry condition.

Little Alfred was laughing, but when he saw his mother pick up an elm switch his smile suddenly vanished. Sally May snatched him up, turned him over her knee, and dusted the seat of his britches.

She turned him loose and stood over him. "You're just being terrible today! I don't know what's gotten into you, but I won't allow a child of mine to be cruel to dumb animals."

(She was referring to Pete there.)

"First you pulled Hank's tail and then you threw poor Pete into the water. That's not nice, young man, and you ought to be ashamed of yourself!"

"Well," Alfred sniffled, "he needed a baff."

"Cats don't bathe in water, Alfred, they wash themselves with their tongues."

"Well . . . his tongue was dirty."

"No, his tongue was not dirty. You were just being mean and cruel, and I've got a new baby in the house and I can't be watching you every minute of the day. If you don't play nice, you'll have to come inside and take a nap."

She started back towards the house. When she passed me, she stopped and scowled. Maybe she noticed that I was, uh, smiling. I mean, tossing Pete into the septic tank ain't exactly my idea of a serious crime. Furthermore, it had been his cousin, Sinister, who had pulverized me the night before.

She shook her finger in my face. "And don't you be giving my child any more ideas about tormenting the cat, Hank McNasty."

HUH? Who, me? Well, hey, I . . .

"I know what you're thinking, and you'd better leave my cat alone. If I hear more yowling, I'll . . . I don't know what I'll do, but you'll be the first to find out."

Yes ma'am.

She stormed back to the house. If she'd known what Little Alfred had on his mind, she wouldn't have left so soon.

CHAPTER FOUR

Another Triumph over the Cat

When Sally May had gone, I turned back to the cat and noticed that he was smirking. I never did like a cat who smirked. I've never even cared for cats who didn't smirk.

I don't like cats.

"What are you smirking about?"

"Hi, Hankie. You got in trouble again, didn't you?"

"Maybe I did and maybe I didn't, but you got throwed in the water. That's what really matters."

Drover was right behind me. "Yeah, that's what really matters."

"How was your swim, Pete? Tell us all about it. Did you enjoy the water or was it a *terrible experience?* We want to know because your unhappiness

33

is the most important thing in the world to us."

"Yeah," said Drover, "and we want to hear all about it."

Pete lifted a front paw and gave it a shake. And he continued to grin, which didn't set too well with me. He was trying to pretend that he had control of the situation, but I knew better.

"It was really very nice, Hankie."

"Oh no it wasn't. You hated it."

"Yeah," said Drover, peeking around my back side, "you hated it and we know you hated it, and since you hated it so bad, we love it."

Pete stood up and stretched. "No, I was surprised how much I enjoyed it." He began slinking our way with his tail stuck straight up in the air. "Oh, I didn't care too much for the water itself, but there were other benefits."

I could hear him purring now. My lips began to twitch as my autonomadic nervous system kicked in and struggled to take over my snarling responses.

"Oh yeah? What so-called other benefits? I don't believe you."

"Well, Hankie, I shouldn't tell you because it would only make you mad."

"Oh yeah?" said Drover.

"Quiet, Drover, I'll handle this." I turned back

to the cat. "Oh yeah? I don't think there were any benefits. I think you hated every second you spent in the water. I think your subterranean mind is seething with anger and thoughts of revenge. Isn't that right?"

He was coming closer, and still smirking. "Oh no, Hankie, those are the crude emotions you might find in dogs, but we cats aren't made that way."

"I have two words to say to that, Pete: *HA, HA!*"

"Yeah," said Drover, "and HA, HA again!"

"Well said, Drover. So there you are, Pete. Four ha-ha's in response to your outrageous lie. As you can see, no one here believes you."

"But it's true, Hankie."

By this time he was right in front of me, rubbing on my front legs and feather-dusting my nose with his tail, which I didn't like.

"Get that tail out of my face, cat."

"Do you want me to tell you the two benefits I received from being thrown in the water?"

I thought seriously about amputating his tail, but decided to postpone it for a moment. "Yes, I'd like to hear that, Kitty, but be quick about it."

"Oh, I will, Hankie. The first benefit was that Sally May came to my rescue."

"Yes, of course she did. You have her completely bluffed out. She doesn't know what a sneaking little weasel you are."

"Um hummm, and the second benefit is that I can do almost *anything* to you now, Hankie, and if you do anything back to me, you'll be in big trouble with Sally May."

HUH?

My ears shot up. My lips curled. A growl began to rumble in my throat.

Pete flicked his tail across my nose. "Isn't this fun, Hankie? You'd probably like to jump right in the middle of me, wouldn't you? But you know what would happen if you did, don't you?"

"You're bluffing, cat, you can't . . . get that tail out of my face!"

"I'm impressed with your self-control, Hankie, but I know a little trick that will just drive you crazy."

"No you don't. Get away and leave me alone! You can't . . ."

"Here, let's try it and see."

He stuck his smirking mug right into my face. Then he hissed and slapped me on the tenderest part of my nose with his claws.

Well, you know me. *Do unto others but don't take trash off the cats.* He had hissed in my face

36

and slapped me across the nose, and that threw his behavior up into the Trash Category.

And what did I do? I just by George buried him!

"REEEEEEER!!"

"Git 'im, Hankie, git 'im!"

I was well on my way to teaching Pete the error of his ways when all at once I heard the back door slam up at the house. Then the yard gate slammed. Then . . . heavy footsteps coming our way.

"All right, Hank, you've done it now! I warned you to leave my cat alone and now . . ."

That was Sally May. She sounded . . . I glanced at Pete who was suddenly limping around in circles and moaning and dragging one back leg behind him. But in spite of his so-called "injuries," he managed to smirk back at me.

"I told you there were benefits, Hankie, but you didn't believe me."

Sally May began shelling us from twenty yards out, and the rocks were falling very close to the mark. In fact, one hit me right in the back.

"Ooooof! She got me! Come on, Drover, it's time to sell out and head for the brush! There's a crazy woman . . . ooooof! . . . coming our way!"

And with that, we went streaking down to the creek where we vanished into the willows and

tamaracks that saved our lives. I had only one
regret about the ... no, I had several regrets
about the incident, but I'd rather not discuss any
of them.

Let's just drop it.

Well, I had taken two direct hits from Sally
May and I was in the process of trying to lick my
wounds, so to speak, when all at once ...

My ears jumped to the Full Alert position. I
had heard an odd noise. I turned to Drover. "Did
you hear something?"

"What?"

"I said, did you hear something?"

"Oh. No, I didn't." But just then he heard it—

a kind of low moan or cry. "Oh yeah, there it is."

We listened. "Holy smokes, Drover, do you suppose Sally May has followed us down into our hiding place? No, wait. She wouldn't have left her baby, and furthermore, she's probably too busy fawning over her stupid cat."

"I thought only deers could fawn."

"Exactly. So it couldn't be her."

"And it wasn't me."

"And it wasn't me."

"And that doesn't leave anybody we know. Maybe it's a deer."

"I doubt that, Drover. Deer don't make the kind of low, moaning sound I'm picking up. Come on, let's slip through the brush and establish a forward position. Stay behind me and don't get hurt."

"You don't need to worry about that."

I went into my Stealthy Crouch Mode and slithered through the brush. I peered out into a small clearing, and there, sitting beside the creek, was a small boy dressed in striped overalls.

It was Little Alfred, and he was crying his little heart out.

Let me pause here to point out that, even though Little Alfred had pulled my tail only hours before, even though he—at the age of

39

four—had turned into an ornery little stinkpot who didn't deserve to have a loyal dog as a friend, in spite of all that, when I saw the boy sitting there alone and crying my wicked old heart just melted.

You talk about cowdog instincts? Well, most of our instincts are directed towards being tough and hardboiled, towards protecting the ranch and doing a job, but fellers, we also have an instinct that responds to a little boy with tears running down his face.

I had to go to him, I couldn't help it. No matter what he'd done, I forgave him because . . .

Don't get me wrong. I'm not saying that I loved the kid. I know, I'd helped raise him and everything, but when you're big and tough and about half-mean, you don't . . .

I liked him, that's all I'm saying. And I cared about him. And by George, if he needed a friend, I was just the dog for the job.

I raised up and started towards him. Drover stayed where he was. "Hank, you'd better keep away from him. He'll pull your tail again and make you yelp."

"Then let him."

"He's mean and naughty."

"Maybe he is, Drover, but he's my boy."

"I don't think anybody else wants him."

"He's my boy, and Duty calls."

I went down to the creek bank and sat down beside Little Alfred and started licking the tears off of his cheeks. He looked up, kind of surprised, and there for a second I didn't know what he would do.

Then he threw his arms around my neck and cried and told me all about his troubles.

CHAPTER FIVE

Running Away
from Home

"**M**y mommy doesn't wuv me anymore," Little Alfred told me as we sat on the creek bank. "She bwought home a new baby and she doesn't care about me. I don't wike her dumb old baby, and I don't wike her anymore either, because she was mean and spanked me."

I listened and wagged my tail. He went on.

"I'm going to wun away fwom home, Hankie, far, far away. I'm never coming back and they'll never see me again. Then they'll wish they had Wittle Alfred back, but Wittle Alfred will be gone, gone, gone away."

I stood up and cleared my throat and began pacing. "Well, I have several points to make, pardner, and since you wanted to know what I thought about all this, here goes.

"In the first place, your ma did in fact bring home a new baby, but that doesn't mean she's stopped caring about you. In the second place, I can testify that you've been something less than a perfect child today, and some of us might even say that you deserved a spanking.

"Don't get me wrong, son. I've had my tail pulled before and it ain't killed me yet, but you've got to understand that those of us with tails don't enjoy tail-twisting as much as other forms of entertainment.

"And as for that business with the cat, I kind of agree with you that your ma went overboard. You and I know that Pete needed a bath anyway, but your ma has strange ideas about cats. She's just built that way and she can't help it.

"In the third place . . ." I turned and was about to sum up my case when . . .

HUH?

He was gone. Little Alfred had vanished!

Drover was still sitting in the brush, a few feet away. "Where did he go?"

"Who?"

"Little Alfred, you dunce! Who else was sitting here just a minute ago?"

43

"I don't know. All I saw was you and Little Alfred, and he left."

"I realize that, Drover, which is why I asked you where he went."

"Oh. Well, he just got up and walked away in the middle of your speech. I guess he got bored."

"I doubt that. I was giving him good, sound, fatherly advice and . . . which way did he go?"

"Well, let's see." He rolled his eyes. "Did he go across the creek or did he go back towards the house? Did he go up the creek or down the creek? I'll be derned, I can't remember."

I lumbered over to where he was sitting and gave him a growl. "You'd better start remembering, son, because taking care of that boy is our primary mission of the day."

"Oh gosh. Well, he . . . he went somewhere, I'm almost sure of that, because if he'd stayed where he was, he'd still be there."

I increased the volume of my growl. "Reach into the huge vacuum of your mind, Drover, and pull out the answer, and be quick about it, because if anything happens to that kid . . ."

"Well, let me think here. He went . . . yes, he did, he went across the creek, Hank, I'm pretty sure he did."

"What? And you just sat there and watched him go?"

"Well . . . sort of. I thought about barking but I've had this sore throat all day and . . ."

"Sore throat! Is that all you can say for yourself?"

"My allergies have been acting up on me." He sneezed. "Kind of hurts my throat to bark."

I shook my head in disbelief. "Drover, do you realize what lies on the other side of this creek?"

"Sand?"

"Yes, sand, but do you realize what lies beyond the sand on the south bank? The Dark Unchanted Forest on the Parnell Ranch! And if Little Alfred gets lost in there, we might never find him again!"

"Gosh."

"Huge trees, Drover, draped with hanging vines. It's dark in there, and scary. On every side, thorny plants and stinging nettles, and no one knows what kind of creatures you might find in there: coyotes, coons, snakes, monsters, bobcats . . ."

"Bobcats! You know, Hank, this leg of mine . . ."

"That's where Little Alfred has gone, Drover, into the Dark Unchanted Forest, and I guess you know what that means."

"Yeah, he was a nice kid in many ways."

"It means that we must prepare ourselves for a very dangerous journey."

"Back to the house, I'll bet."

I stared at the runt. "No, not back to the house, into the woods. For you see, Drover, what we have here is The Case of the Lost Child in the Dark Unchanted Forest."

"I was afraid of that."

"And the task of finding Little Alfred has fallen upon our shoulders."

Drover pushed himself up and began limping around. "Boy, speaking of shoulders, this old leg of mine is sure giving me fits."

"Never mind your leg. We've got a mission to make, a very dangerous and important . . ."

"Oh my leg! Hank, I just don't think I can make it, maybe you'd better go on without me, I'll try to crawl back to the house and sound the alarm!"

"You'd actually do such a thing? You'd let me go into the Dark Unchanted Forest all alone?"

"Oh heck yes, I wouldn't worry about you, 'cause you're big and strong."

"That's true."

"And you're Head of Ranch Security."

"Yes, I am."

"And you're not afraid of anything."

"Yes . . . well, that might be a slight overstatement. Actually, I wouldn't mind having you . . ."

He started backing away. "And I'll just slip on back to the ranch and sound the alarm, and you can find Little Alfred and that'll be the end of it."

"Now hold on, Drover, let's talk this . . ."

"Bye, Hank, and good luck with the snakes and monsters!"

"Wait . . . Drover, come back here!"

Too late. The little mutt disappeared into the brush, and I didn't notice that his so-called bad leg slowed him down very much.

So there I was, all alone. All at once I noticed a restless wind moaning in the tops of the trees. It was a damp wind, out of the southeast, and overhead dark clouds were beginning to gather.

This was the stormy season, and unless I missed my guess, we were in for some bad weather. A shiver ran down my backbone. I wasn't looking forward to this job, and . . .

Come to think of it, *my* leg was beginning to act up on me. I walked around on it and tested it out.

By George, it was pretty sore, didn't know what I'd done to make it hurt so bad, but all at once it started shooting terrible hot pains all through my . . . and it suddenly occurred to me that it would be foolish of me to go off on a dangerous . . .

No question about it, fellers, I was pretty badly crippled up, and the worst thing a guy can do is to go off on an important mission with a bum leg; I mean, you run the risk of messing up the whole deal, and although I hated the idea of . . .

Holy smokes, that limp was getting worse by the second. I mean, you talk about pain! And I knew in my deepest heart that if Little Alfred had been there he would have advised me to go on back to the ranch and take it easy and give that old leg a chance to heal up, because . . .

I started back to the house. I was sure the boy would find his way home.

Somebody would find him.

Kids don't just disappear.

Surely . . .

I heard Sally May's voice in the distance. "Alfred? Alfred? Where are you? Come home!"

I stopped in my tracks. I looked up at the dark sky. I looked back at the dark forest. I listened to the moan of the wind. I sure wanted to go home.

But dern it, I just couldn't do it! No sir, my little pal was lost out there and he needed me, and even though I didn't want the job of finding him, there was nobody else to do it.

I turned around, made a run for the creek, dived into the water, swam across, and came out

on the other side. My old heart was banging like a bass drum and I could feel little needles of fear pricking the back of my neck, but I tried to put it all out of my mind.

I trotted up and down the creek bank, sniffing the sand and looking for Little Alfred's tracks. Even though Pete had done some damage to the leathery exterior portion of my nose, the interior mechanisms were still functioning at full capacity, and it shouldn't surprise anybody that I picked up the scent right away.

I mean, my nose is a pretty impressive piece of equipment. Not only is it the most striking feature of my face, but it's also . . .

That was odd. *Two* sets of tracks! I bent down and gave the ground a thorough sniffing. One set of tracks had been made by Little Alfred, and it went off in the direction of the Dark Unchanted Forest. The other set of tracks led off in the same direction, almost as, though . . .

HUH?

Those were bobcat tracks. Sinister the Bobcat was on the prowl. Holy smokes, that pain in my leg . . .

I lifted my head and tried to swallow. My mouth was dry all of a sudden. I didn't know whether bobcats ate little boys or not, but the tracks in the sand suggested that one of them had just followed Little Alfred into the woods, and unless I did something pretty fast . . .

I didn't stop to think it through. I headed south in a dead run and went plunging into the Great Unknown, barking at the top of my lungs and trying to warn my little pal.

"Alfred, watch out, son! There's a bobcat on your trail!"

CHAPTER SIX

A Witch
in the Forest

I entered the Dark Unchanted Forest near the spot where that big cottonwood tree sits. You know the one: great big tree with gnarled limbs that reach up like a hand, and there's a fresh scar running down the trunk where the tree was struck by lightning.

Maybe you don't remember the tree because, well, maybe you haven't seen it. Okay.

But the important thing is that I remembered it. I remembered it because I had seen it many times before and because I studied it again to be double sure that I would remember it, because once you get into the Dark Unchanted Forest, you get turned around and lose your sense of direction.

Going into that place was easy. Getting out was the problem, and before a guy goes plunging into it he'd better have a few landmarks memorized.

I'd be the first to admit that a tree wasn't the best landmark in the world, since it sort of follows from simple logic that a forest is full of trees, but what kind of landmarks do you suppose you'd find in a place full of trees? *Trees!*

So I memorized every detail of that big cottonwood tree . . . and hoped that there weren't a thousand more trees just like it.

And having done that, I put my nose to the ground, picked up the trail, and followed it into the forest.

We don't have many forests in our country, which is mostly rolling prairie with caprocks and canyons. Here and there you find a heavily wooded area down along the creek, don't you see, so you might say that I hadn't spent much time training for rescue work in a forested situation.

Myself, I'm more of a prairie dog—not one of those little rodents that digs holes in the ground. They're called prairie dogs too, even though they're not dogs at all. No, I'm a prairie dog in that I prefer working in open country where I can see for miles in all directions.

I dig holes in the ground every now and then,

but I've never been a rodent. You couldn't pay me to be a rodent.

The point is, I prefer the wide open spaces. Heavily wooded areas give me the creeps because I can't see what lies ahead or to the sides, and I have this active imagination that is very good at turning bushes and shadows into ... well, monsters.

Fellers, once I entered that dark spooky forest, I saw more monsters in five minutes than I'd seen in my entire life. You never saw so many monsters! I saw three Leaf Monsters, four Bush Monsters, two Shadow Monsters, and seven Tree Monsters.

Which sort of gets me back to what I was saying about training. If a guy has trained in a spooky forest situation, he learns that even though these monsters look scary, the stastics ... sassticksicks ... sta-tis-tics, the statistics show that they don't often eat dogs.

And once he knows this, he can go on about his business without being distracted. In other words, he can follow the scent.

What I'm driving at in sort of a roundabout way is that I got so busy dodging forest monsters that, dern the luck, I lost the scent.

As you might expect, we have a response to that

problem. When we lose a scent, we turn around and backtrack until we pick up the scent again.

I turned around all right, but once I turned around, I found myself . . . well, turned around, you might say, and it's a well known fact that you can't backtrack if you've lost the track and don't know which way is back.

All at once I found myself basically lost. I had lost the scent, the trail, my sense of direction, my sense of well being, my courage, my confidence, my curiosity, and my devotion to duty. But most of all, I had lost all desire to be where I was.

Fellers, I was lost and scared, surrounded by forest monsters and strange sounds—hoots and tweets and cheeps, twitters and crackles and slithers, coos and moans and sighs, whispers and lispers and laughter.

Why didn't I leave the forest? There's a very simple explanation for that. A guy can't leave what he doesn't like unless he knows where to find something better. And I didn't.

Completely lost and turned around is what we're talking about here, an important mission so badly botched that I would dearly love to drop the whole subject. I mean, it's embarrassing to be the Head of . . .

Better mush on with the story.

Okay. I was lost, I admit that. And with no better plan in mind I chose one direction out of the hat, so to speak, and went stumbling through the vines and so forth, hoping that in the process of stumbling I might stumble onto a more coherent plan of action.

I hadn't gone far when, all at once, I thought I heard a voice. At first I dismissed it as just another of the many spooky sounds of the forest. But then I heard it again, and this time I couldn't dismiss it.

"Oh my goodness!" said the voice. "Who should be coming through the forest but Hank the Rabbit!"

"Huh? Who said that?"

"I did. I think I did. Or maybe I didn't. It depends on what you heard."

"I heard someone say something about Hank the Rabbit."

"Oh yes, 'twas I who said that."

"Yeah, well, there's a couple of things we ought to get straight right away. Number One, I can't see you and it makes me uncomfortable to carry on a conversation with nobody."

"If you're talking with nobody, and if nobody hears, then nobody cares, so it really doesn't matter, does it?"

"Well uh . . ." There was something familiar about that voice. Hadn't I heard it before? Seemed to me that I had, but I couldn't place it. "I'd feel more comfortable if I could see you. Tell me where you are."

"I'm here and you're there, and we don't know any more than we did before, so what's the point of knowing where we are?"

"I'd like to look you in the eyes, is what I'm saying."

"Well of course you would. Find me and you'll find my eyes. Or find my eyes and I won't be far behind."

"Yeah, but . . ."

"But you can't find either one—I or eyes—so I will look you in the eyes while your eyes look for mine."

I sat down and peered into the gloomy vine-covered gloominess of the forest. Couldn't see anybody.

"You know, you have a way of confusing words, and it seems to me that I met somebody once who talked that way."

"Oh my goodness, who could I be?"

"Well, I don't know. That's what I was fixing to ask."

"Go right ahead and ask."

"Okay. Who could you be?"

"Well, I could be a tree if I had roots. Or I could be a cloud if I could float. Or I could be a dream if I could sleep. But I can't and I'm not, and I'm only who I am instead of who I could be."

"All right, I guess that sort of narrows it down. Who are you?"

"I hate simple questions. They require simple answers, and whoever I am, I'm not simple. I simply can't answer your question."

This was getting me nowhere. "All right, then let's move to my second point."

"Oh no, how dull! Let's skip the second and go on to the third."

"Huh? No, I don't have a third point. Just two."

"All things have three parts: the first half, the second half, and the third half which we didn't know was there. But it is there, so skip the second part and go to the third."

"Well . . . all right, I guess . . . my second point, which is the same as your third part . . ."

"Now you're getting in the spirit!"

". . . is that you called me 'Hank the Rabbit,' and I'm not a rabbit, see. I'm a dog, Hank the Cowdog, Head of Ranch Security."

"Oh, I know all that! But I like Hank the

Rabbit better than Hank the Cowdog, so I will call you Hank the Rabbit."

"Well, whatever you . . ." Suddenly the pieces of the puzzle began falling into place. I remembered running into somebody once who had called me Hank the Rabbit. "Say, I think I just figgered out who you are! You're Madame Moonshine, the witchy little owl."

I waited for her to answer but she didn't. There was a long throbbing silence.

"Madame? Madame Moonshine? Speak to me."

"Rubbish!"

"You're the one who cured me of Eye-Crosserosis."

"Double rubbish sassafras horseradish balderdash!"

"And that explains why you've been talking in circles. Shucks, you're a witch."

"Yes, I'm a witch but also a switch."

"Huh?"

"Where would you look to find a switch?"

"Well, let's see . . . a switch . . . hmmm. In a tree?"

"A switch in a tree, a witch that is me. Make the switch and find a witch, trah-lah, trah-lah, trah-lah."

Hmmm. All the evidence was pointing . . .

maybe if I raised my eyes from ground level . . . heck, I'd been looking for her on the ground but . . .

I raised my eyes and studied the circle of trees all around me, and . . . mercy, there she was, hanging upside-down from a vine that was draped over a big hackberry tree.

"Ah ha! There you are. I've found you at last."

She smiled—upside-down, which was a little peculiar since an upside-down smile is about the same as a frown.

"I knew you could do it!" she said. "You not only found who I am but where I am. Oh Hank, you're such a clever rabbit and I do need your help."

"I'm still not a rabbit, Madame, but I'd be glad to help you if I can, because to tell you the truth, I'm in kind of a jam myself."

This was a real struck of loke, me running into Madame Moonshine, because I had a feeling that she could find Little Alfred and help me save him from the bobcat.

CHAPTER SEVEN

Disorientation

So there I was in the Dark Unchanted Forest. I was lost, but I had found Madame Moonshine hanging upside-down by one foot from a vine.

"Well, what sort of help do you need, Madame?"

"Oh Hank, I have a dilemma here. I've caught my foot in this vine and I'm hanging downside-up."

"Hmmm. I would have said 'upside-down.'"

"Picky picky! It's all the same, isn't it? Downside-up and upside-down, wrongside-up and rightside-down, backside-up and topside-down! The problem is the same, and the problem is that I'm backwards."

"Yes, I see what you mean. You do look sort of

backwards, hanging up there. I noticed that right away."

"How clever! But that is only the first half of the three-halved problem. There are two more halves to my dilemma."

"Well shucks, Madame, if I was a witch like you, I'd use my special powers to get myself unhooked."

"No you wouldn't."

"Huh? Well . . . yeah, I think I would. Why not? If you've got special powers, you might as well use them."

"But what if the power works backwards? There is always that danger with power. If I am backwards, maybe my power is backwards too, and my goodness, we don't know what might happen then! I wouldn't dare try it . . . unless . . ."

"Unless what?"

She looked at me with her big upside-down eyes. "Unless you were absolutely convinced that I should, and then I might. Or might not, depending upon my mood."

"I think it's worth a shot, Madame."

"Do you now? And tell me again what your title is?"

I sat up straight and lifted my chin a few inches. "Head of Ranch Security, ma'am."

"My goodness, the Head of Ranch Security! How could we go wrong if we're in the presence of the Head of Ranch Security?"

I smiled to myself. "A lot of people ask that same question, ma'am, and the answer I always give 'em is that with me around, there ain't much that can go wrong. Let's give it a shot."

"Very well, if you're sure."

"Go for it."

She closed her eyes and mumbled some magic words. Let's see if I can remember what they were:

Topsy-turvy, downside-up, vertigo and
    spirally.
I wish, O Power, you'd intervene: reverse
    the scene entirely.

Sounded like pretty good words to me. The only problem was that, all at once, I heard a rush of wind and felt myself flying through the air; and the next thing I knew, I was hanging upside-down from the same vine as Madame Moonshine!

She stared at me and blinked her eyes. "My goodness, what have we done?"

"Well, we've changed the scene entirely, Madame, but I think it came out backwards."

She clicked her tongue. "I was afraid of that.

Oh Hank, I shouldn't have listened to you. I knew better. But on the other hand . . ." She rolled her head around, funny how she could do that, and looked at me with her big owl eyes. "On the other hand, I've been in worse places before."

"You have?"

"Oh yes. And now that you're up here with me, I don't feel upside-down anymore."

"You don't?"

"Oh no. We can pretend that everything else is upside-down and that we're right-side up, can't we?"

"Well . . . uh . . ."

"And who knows, maybe we are. There are so many strange things happening these days. Maybe my backwards power made the whole forest turn topsy-turvy, and now we're the only objects that are right."

"No ma'am, I don't think so. I think we're hanging upside-down and I'm completely disoriented."

"What's wrong with that?"

"Well . . . I don't like it, is all I can tell you. Let me see if I can explain it."

At that point, as strange as it may sound, my being upside-down and everything, I sang her a little song.

Disorientation

Now, Madame Moonshine, tell me truly,
If your view of life's unruly,
How can you figger it out?
See, my down-side is up, I'm confused as a pup,
I can't distinguish up from about.

I'm told the world spins 'round the sun,
What's here is here, what's done is done,
And I can accept that as true.
But the normal world looks strange enough
    without this bunch of other stuff,
I'm backwards, Madame, how about you?

Disorientation
It's a revelation
It will turn your head around.
'Cause it's hard to keep your feet on the ground,
When you're hanging upside-down.

Then Madame Moonshine sang back to me.
Here's how it went:

Now, early in our history
The world was cloaked in mystery
But two sides began to take shape:

The up-side was up and the down-side was
    down.
A simple logic hard to escape.

But why should simple logic rule
This universe, this whirlpool
That's vast beyond our wildest surmise?
You've no idea what might could be, you're
    just a dog and cannot see
That certainty in life's the real surprise.

Disorientation
It's a revelation
It will turn your head around.
'Cause it's hard to keep your feet on the
    ground,
When you're hanging upside-down.

Well, that was pretty good so I sang the next
verse and she did the one after that.

That's well and good but I say that
A dog's a dog and a cat's a cat
A blackbird's black and a bluebird is blue.
But when they're walking upside-down, the
    ground's sky and the sky's the ground,
I tell you, Madame, I am confused.

The answer, Hank, is plain to see:
You think you're you, you think I'm me,
But sometimes we're not what you think.
There's a lesson to be learned from reality
    upturned:
That everything can change in a blink.

Disorientution
It's a revolution
It will turn your head around.
'Cause it's hard to keep your feet on the
    ground,
When you're hanging upside-down.

"You sing pretty well, Madame," I said when we were done with the song.

"Well, thank you, Hank. And you don't do badly yourself. You see, disorientation isn't such a bad thing after all."

"I said you sing well, Madame. I didn't say that I agreed with everything you said."

"In other words . . ."

"In other words, hanging upside-down from a tree is for the birds."

"Maybe that's what it is! I'm a bird, you know."

"That's true, hadn't thought of that, but the point is that my paws have no business pointing towards the sky, and if it's all the same to you, I'd like to get these old feet back on the ground."

"Yes, I see. Oh dear."

"What do you mean, 'Oh dear?'"

"I mean, oh dear, that brings up the third half of my problem. The first half was that I found myself hanging upside-down from this tree. The second half was that I suspected my power might work backwards."

"And the third half?"

"Yes, there's always a third half, isn't there? The third half is that, only moments before you arrived, two very hungry-looking coyotes were sitting at the base of this tree."

"Hmmm, yes, I see what you mean."

"And they gave me the feeling that, were I to fall back to the ground, they would snatch me up in their jaws and eat me in two bites."

"That would make a guy feel a little happier about hanging upside-down from a tree, wouldn't it?"

"I thought so. So there are the three halves of my problem. Now tell me about yours."

Holy smokes, I'd almost forgotten about Little Alfred and the bobcat! In fact, you might even say that I had *completely* forgotten about them.

I told her all about it. "And I've got to get

down from here and find that boy before something happens to him. I'd never forgive myself
if . . . Madame, if you could help me find the boy,
I'd sure be grateful."

"Oh dear. Let me think. If we work ourselves
loose and fall back to the ground, we might be
eaten by savages. But as long as we remain here,
my powers will be backwards and I can't be of any
help to you. We do have our problems, don't we?"

"So it seems, Madame so it seems."

"And what do you suggest we do?"

I studied on that for a minute. "Madame, as I
was coming up to this tree I didn't run into any
fresh coyote tracks. And looking in all directions
from this observation point, I still don't see any
sign of coyotes."

"Yes?"

"And while I'm naturally soft-spoken and mod-
est about my talents, I might mention in passing
that tracking and observation are two of the many
things a dog must do well if he plans to make a
career in the security business, and at the risk of
thumping my own tub, so to speak, I might also
mention that I'm pretty salty at both of them."

"And?"

"And my preliminary scans have come up
with negative results, leading me to suspect that

the alleged coyotes have left the country and gone on to better things."

"You're quite sure about that?"

"Oh yes ma'am. Preliminary scans aren't quite as thorough and reprehensive as your complete scans, don't you see, but based on the evidence at hand, I'd have to say that the immediate area is clear of . . ."

At that very moment, two heads appeared from behind a bush near the base of the tree. Both heads were attached to bodies, and both showed the usual characteristics we look for in positive IDs of . . . coyotes, you might say.

Madame Moonshine swiveled her head in my direction. "Did you want to finish your sentence?"

"Uh . . . no thanks, I was about done anyway."

"Do you see what I see?"

"Let me emphasize that preliminary scans are often faulty and . . ."

"Am I wrong or are they coyotes?"

"They are, uh, the alleged coyotes, I would say, which means we're getting some faulty data on our . . ."

"Do you suppose that they would eat one or both of us, if given the opportunity?"

"Yes ma'am, in a New York minute. It happens that I've had a little experience with those guys, couple of drunken brothers named Rip and Snort, and I'm sorry to report that they're double-tough and always hungry."

"Oh dear. What shall we do?"

"Oh, let's just hang around for a while and see what happens."

CHAPTER EIGHT

Working Some Hoodoo on Rip and Snort

The brothers looked up at us with their yellow eyes sparkling. Snort licked his chops, which was not a good sign.

"Uh! Snort see two bird now in tree. Before, Snort only seeing one bird."

Rip nodded his head.

Snort went on. "One bird plus one bird make how many bird?" Rip grinned and shrugged. "Snort think maybe one bird plus one bird make *two bird*. Two bird with one stone make good deal."

"Uh!" said Rip, nodding his head and licking his chops.

"We gottum two coyote. We gottum two bird. We no gottum one stone."

"Uh!" said Rip, shaking his head and licking his chops. He was pretty definite about licking his chops.

"Little bird, owl. Big bird have funny look, not feathers-wearing or wings-having. Have two ear and long nose, not like bird."

"Uh!" said Rip.

"Snort first dibs on big bird. Rip first dibs on little owl."

"UH UH!"

"Rip and Snort share big bird, eat first. Then eat little owl."

"Uh." Rip nodded on that.

Madame Moonshine and I exchanged glances. She grinned and blinked her eyes. "It sounds as though they want you to go first."

"Yeah, well what they want and what they get are two different propositions. Let me talk to them. I happen to be fluent in their language.

"It sounds like Ignorish to me."

"No ma'am, it's your basic coyolect diote... eh, coyote dialect, that is, which is a branch off the tree of Universal Doglish."

"I see."

"And I happen to be fluent in all your Doglish

dialects, plus I've had some dealings with these guys before. I just might be able to make a deal with 'em."

"If the deal is to offer me for supper, I hope you'll decline."

"Well sure. I mean, I hope you don't think . . ." Actually, I had considered . . . that is, I never would have thought of such an outrageous plan. No way. We were in this thing together.

I turned to the brothers. "Afternoon, guys. What do you reckon this weather's going to do?"

"UH?" They went into a huddle and whispered back and forth. Then Snort said, "That you, Hunk?"

"Yup, the same old charming devil you've done business with many times, Snort, and it's great to see you again."

They held another conference. "Brother say, not so great for Hunkbird if we eat Hunkbird."

"That's a good point, I hadn't really . . . of course, you realize that I'm not actually a bird."

"Uh?"

"It's true. I'm not a bird and never was, and you've probably got your taste buds all tuned up for a bird dinner, so this will come as a big disappointment to you. I'm not a bird, see."

They talked it over. Snort shook his head. "Rip and Snort not believe big lies. Dog not hang from tree, only bird. Hunk dogbird."

"Yes, well, I can see how you might . . . actually, I can explain the whole thing if you've got a few minutes."

They shook their heads and stared at me with their brutish yellow eyes. "Not having few minutes. Also not give a hoot if dog or bird or bird dog. Rip and Snort eat whatsomever, not care."

"Well sure, but then again, you're probably asking yourselves, 'Gee whiz, how do you reckon old Hank climbed up in that tree?'"

"Not wondering 'gee whiz.' Not care."

"Of course you care, Snort. Furthermore, you're probably wishing that you and Rip could crawl up that tree over there and play Bat, just as we are here."

"What means, 'play Bat'?"

"Oh, you know, playing Bat. Remember all the warm and wonderful days of your childhood? Your ma was there, and your brothers and sisters. It was a bright, warm afternoon in the spring, just about like today, and you saw a bat hanging from a tree, and oh, how you wished that you could be a bat and hang upside-down from a tree! Remember?"

They whispered back and forth. Then Snort said, "Bat mean like baseball bat?"

"No, no, you don't understand. A bat is a small-ish, mouse-looking creature with long wings."

"Mouse not have wings. Mouse have legs."

"I know that, Snort. What I'm saying . . ."

"Coyote eat many mouse. Mouse not have wings."

"I agree, you're exactly right, but I was trying to steer the conversation into bats."

"Coyote not give hoot for baseball."

"These bats have nothing to do with baseball. What we're trying to establish here . . ."

"Coyote not give hoot for trying to establish."

I stared at him. "You have a closed mind, Snort, did you realize that? Here I'm trying to give you a little education and expand your . . ."

"Coyote not give hoot for nothing! Only like eat and drink and sing, oh boy!"

I turned to Madame Moonshine. "This isn't working."

"I wasn't going to say anything, but I had begun to wonder."

"Those guys are so dumb, it's like talking to a couple of stumps."

"Then it appears that we shall be eaten."

"Not yet." I studied the two savages down below and tried to come up with a plan. They had put their heads together and appeared to be tuning up for a song. "Madame, they're fixing to sing the Coyote Sacred Hymn and National Anthem. It's an old coyote tradition. When they're done singing, they eat."

"Oh dear."

"We've got to work fast. Now, I know it's risky to use your backwards power, but before, when you told it to reverse the scene, it yanked me up here in the tree. Maybe . . ."

"Yes, I see what you mean. Maybe, if I try it again, it will sweep them off the ground and hang them in a tree."

"Exactly. And then we'll try to work ourselves loose and get the heck out of here."

"What a marvelous plan!"

I gave her a wink. "Hey, you're running around with the Head of Ranch Security. I didn't get this job strictly on my good looks. Let's give it a shot."

"Very well." She closed her eyes and concentrated. Then her eyes popped open. "Oh, dear!"

"Oh dear what?"

"I can't remember the words!"

"Well, make up some new ones. And hurry."

"I hate to experiment with incantations. Sometimes they backfire."

"Yeah, but if we don't do something pretty quick, we won't have any backs left to fire."

"Very well. Here we go." She squeezed her eyes shut and said the magic words:

Topsy-turvy, rickets scurvy, barley rye and
    wheatly,
Backwards power, sweet and sour, reverse
    this scene completely!

Now all we had to do was wait for the power to . . .

Well I'll be a son of a gun. You know what the power did? Do you think it swept Rip and Snort off the ground and hung them up in a grapevine? Do you think it saved us from becoming coyote bait?

No sir. Instead of reversing the whole entire scene, as we had hoped, it zeroed in on Rip and Snort's song and, dern the luck, made them sing all their words backwards! Here's how it went:

Coyote worthless a just me,
Moon the at howling me,
Holler and sing to like me,
Loon a as crazy me.

Duties or job want not me,
School Sunday or church no,

Coyote worthless a just me,
Fool nobody's ain't me but.

Beat anything I ever saw. But you know what? I couldn't see that it made much difference. The song sounded just as bad backwards as it did forwards, which is really saying something. Furthermore, I don't think Rip and Snort even knew they had just sung their national anthem backwards.

"Oh dear," said Madame Moonshine. "I think I missed again."

"Yes, it appears that you did, Madame, which is a piece of bad luck for us."

"Yes, because you might have noticed that it's begun to rain."

"Say, you're right, it has started to rain. That's okay, these pastures could use the moisture."

"I'm sure that's true, but I don't think that *we* need the moisture."

"What do you mean?"

"The rain is wetting my foot, and unless I'm badly mistaken, my foot is beginning to slip out of the vine."

HUH?

If her foot slipped out of the vine, then she would most likely . . . and if HER foot was slipping

loose, the chances were pretty good that MY
foot . . .

*Holy smokes, my foot was slipping out of the
vine!* And fellers, if it pulled loose, my life
expectancy could be measured by the time it would
take for me to free-fall from the tree to the ground.

Short, in other words. Real short.

"Madame, I have one last idea."

"Oh my goodness, I do hope it's not your last!"

"Well, if it doesn't work, it will be. We're fixing
to fall into a crocodile pit."

"Yes, and I'm so annoyed at my power! It was
working so well last week, I just don't understand . . ."

I hated to butt in on a witch, but I could feel
my foot slipping out of the vine. We only had a
few seconds left.

"Listen, Madame, here's the plan. On the count
of three, we'll push ourselves out of the vine."

"On the count of three, yes."

"We have to fall at the same time, see?"

"Same time, yes."

"When you hit the ground, jump to your feet
so that you're standing upright."

"Jump to my . . . upright, yes, go on."

"When you're upright, your power ought to
work again, right?"

"One would hope so, wouldn't one?"

"And then you make a wish."

"A wish. One wish. I think I've got it."

"Okay, ready to push off?"

"Ready as I'll ever be."

"One! Two!"

"Hank?"

"Huh?"

"Was there any particular wish I was supposed to make?"

Holy cats, I'd almost forgotten the most impointant parnt, important point!

"Yes, of course, I was going to wait until the last . . . never mind. Okay, the wish. You will wish that Rip and Snort be hungry for nothing but *cat*."

"Cat? I don't think I understand."

"Never mind, I'll explain it all later. Ready? One! Two! And for Pete's sake, get it right this time! Three! Charge, bonzai!"

I'm not going to reveal at this point whether Madame Moonshine's power worked or if we were eaten alive in the Pit of the Hungry Crocodiles. If I did, you might not read the next chapter. But now, because I've withheld crucial information, you simply must go on and read it.

CHAPTER NINE

Eaten Alive
by Crocodiles

As you might have guessed by now, we were eaten alive by the hungry crocodiles.

Beat anything I ever saw.

Boy, were those guys hungry!

Of course, that sure messes up the story. What do you do and where do you go after something like that happens, and the story ain't but partway done?

I guess we'll just have to shut her down and find something else to do. I hate it, but I don't know what else to tell you.

Except that I'm sort of pulling your leg, so to speak, and playing an ornery little prank. Ho, ho, ho!

See, I knew you'd be all worried and scared

and sitting on the edge of your chair, and I thought it would be fun to . . . I guess you probably figgered it out without me.

Where was I? Oh yes. Madame Moonshine and I had just fallen out of the tree, into the Enormous Gloomy Bottomless Pit of Hungry Crocodiles, and you were wondering if her magic power worked on the croc . . . coyotes, actually.

Well, I don't know. We'll just have to see. Here's what happened—the whole entire truth this time, no fooling around.

We hit the ground with a thud. Two thuds, actually. THUD! THUD! Rip and Snort weren't expecting us to drop in on them that way, don't you see, and our sudden appearance startled them for a couple of seconds, which gave us time to get into position.

I leaped to my feet and yelled at Madame Moonshine to leap to her feet. "Get up, Madame, feap to your leet!"

"What?"

"Leap to your feet!"

"Oh yes, my feet." She placed her wings on the ground and tried to push herself up. "Oh my goodness, I landed right on my fanny, and it hurts!"

"Never mind your fanny. Get up and say the words before those guys make hash out of us!"

By this time Rip and Snort had recovered from the shock, and big nasty smiles were rippling across their mouths. "Uh! Now we have big supper, oh boy!"

"Hurry, Madame, the words!"

She struggled to her feet and gave her head a shake. "The words, the words, oh dear, what were they?"

"Cat."

"Cat, of course, how forgetful of me."

The coyote brothers licked their chops and started towards us. Madame Moonshine closed her eyes and started muttering:

Power power, rain and shower, spider
    webs and this and that,
Make these ruthless savages hungry for
    a bat.

I couldn't believe my ears. "NOT A BAT, A CAT!"

She stared at me and blinked her eyes. "Did I say bat?"

"You certainly did."

"My goodness. I meant to say cat. I don't work well under pressure."

The brothers were moving towards us, a wall

of gleaming yellow eyes and long white teeth and raised hackles. "One last chance, Madame. See if you can make a correction."

"I don't like this pressure! I simply hate doing spells before a crowd."

"Hurry!"

"Oh, all right!" She closed her eyes. "Power, power, I said bat but I meant . . ."

Too late. Snort grabbed her up in his jaws, but at the last second, she yelled out the right word. "Cat! Cat! Oh my goodness, cat!"

By that time Rip had jumped into the middle of me, and before I had time to fight back, he had bedded me down and was standing astraddle of me. I'm not sure fighting back would have done much good anyway. I mean, those guys lived on the wild side, and their idea of good clean fun was to go out and beat up on badgers and get sprayed by skunks.

You could bite 'em and kick 'em and scratch 'em, throw dirt in their eyes and chew on their ears, spit on 'em and yell at 'em and hit 'em between the eyes with a bodark club, and all it would do was make 'em a little madder.

I could see all thirty-seven of Rip's teeth. He had an odd number, see, because several had been knocked out in fights. Boy, they were just about the longest and sharpest teeth I'd ever seen, and I didn't like the way they decorated his smile.

He flicked out his tongue, swept it around the right side of his drooling lips, and then took it all the way back across his mouth and mopped up the left side.

And then he said, "UH!" Which sounded pretty threatening to me.

"Now Rip, don't do anything you might . . . let's talk this thing . . . tell you what, we might work out a . . ."

I didn't know how Madame Moonshine was doing, but my deal was looking worse by the second. Rip gave a yip and a howl and clamped his jaws around my throat, and fellers, I thought my lights were fixing to go out for the last time.

But suddenly he stopped.

He raised up and made a sour face. He spit several times and said, "Uhhhh!" I lifted my head to check on Madame Moonshine. Snort had her in his huge enormous terrible toothy mouth and seemed about ready to chew her up into small bites.

But then he spit her out on the ground. Snort looked at Rip and Rip looked at Snort, and they both had puzzled expressions on their faces.

"Snort not want owl."

"Uh," said Rip.

"Snort hungry for . . . BAT!"

Oh no! Madame had messed up the spell, it wasn't going to work, all my planning had gone to . . .

But then Rip shook his head and said, "Uh-uh!"

Snort stared at his brother. "Snort not want bat?"

"Uh-uh."

"Uh. Maybeso Snort want . . . rat?"

"Uh-uh!"

"Uh. Then maybeso Snort want . . . cat?"

Rip jumped up and down. "Uh huh!"

Good old Rip. Maybe he wasn't too bright, but at least he knew the difference between a cat and a bat.

Snort came lumbering over to me and stuck his long sharp nose right in my face. "Rip and Snort not want eat Hunkbird and little owl. Hunkbird and little owl taste bad. Rip and Snort want cat to eat!"

"A cat? Well, I . . . that does sound delicious, doesn't it?"

"Hunkbird find cat for Rip and Snort or Rip and Snort get mad, tear up whole world, berry big madness."

I pushed myself up off the grass. "All right,

Snort, you've got yourself a deal. Now you guys just back off and give us some air and we'll see if we can find you a cat."

"Uh!" they said in unison.

"Let's see, what kind of cat are you hungry for, Snort? How about a little bitty skinny scrawny cat?" They shook their heads. "No. Well, how about one that's medium-sized, not too big and not too little?"

They shook their heads. "Rip and Snort want great big fat cat, greater biggest fattest cat in whole world!"

"In the whole world, huh? That's asking a lot, Snort, and if you ask me, you're being a little greedy."

"Ha! Snort not give a hoot for asking you."

"All right, whatever you say. If you want a great big fat cat, we'll see if we can find you one."

"Better find one or Snort put big hurt on Hunkbird."

I went over to Madame Moonshine. She was lying on the grass and hadn't moved a muscle since Snort had spit her out.

"Madame? Are you all right?"

One eye popped open. "I have never been treated like this before! The brute, the oaf, the unspeakable wretch!"

"I know what you mean. I had one on me too."

"The lout! The barbarian! The cannibal!"

"Get up, Madame, we still have one job left to do. We've got to find Little Alfred."

"I don't know any Little Alfreds and I'm all upset, and I'm of a mind to put a spell on those two unspeakable brutes that . . ."

I whispered my plan in her ear. Her other eye popped open. A smile formed on her beek . . . beke . . . biek . . . beak . . . how do you spell beeke? Formed on her beak, I guess that's how you spell it, but who cares anyway?

She jumped to her feet. "On second thought, I think I can find your Little Alfred." She threw her head back and closed her eyes and went into deep concentration. "Oh vapors, oh foggy darkness, oh penetrating powers! I see him now, huddled in a shallow cave . . . frightened, alone, wet and cold, crying. And down below . . . a hungry beast is waiting."

"Is it a cat? A bobcat?"

There was a moment of silence. "Is it a cat? Search, powers, and tell me. Yes, it is a cat. And in a tree nearby . . . two buzzards sit huddled on a limb . . . waiting . . . waiting for the terrible deed." She came out of her trance. "We must hurry. Follow me."

I turned to the cannibals. "All right, boys, we've got us a cat located, a great big huge enormous fat cat—with a stub tail."

"Rip and Snort not give a hoot about tail. Hungry for cat!"

"Well, this one's liable to be pretty tough. I hope you can handle him."

"Ha! Rip and Snort not scared of cat. Eat cat in two bites, like june bug!"

"Sounds all right to me, guys. Let's go!"

And with that, we followed Madame Moonshine through the Dark Unchanted Forest. Somewhere in the darkness and the rain, Little Alfred was in bad need of some help.

I only hoped that we weren't too late.

CHAPTER TEN

Rip and Snort Defend Their World Championship Title

What a gloomy day it was! Rain, drizzle, fog, thunder, lightning, the whole nine yards. And what a gloomy place that forest was!

I couldn't wait to wrap this case up and get back to the old prairie country. That forest gave me the creeps, and it didn't help at all that I had two cannibals behind me. I mean, they had their taste buds set on a cat supper, but I didn't know how long that would last.

Never turn your back on a cannibal. That's one of the basic rules we follow in the security business, and it's pretty good advice for anyone.

You might want to jot that down. *Never turn your back on a cannibal.*

Anyway, we went plunging through the gloomy forest. Madame Moonshine was in the lead, hopping along and sometimes flying a few feet at a time. That's the usual traveling pattern for your burrowing owls, don't you see, only you very seldom see them outside of a prairie dog town.

All at once Madame Moonshine stopped and held up one wing. I stopped and the brothers plowed into me.

"Well, excuse me!" I said.

"Hunk get out of trail before Rip and Snort stomp mudhole in middle of back."

"Shhhh!" Madame Moonshine motioned for us to knock off the noise and to come up to the bush where she was standing. Rip and Snort bulled their way past me and stepped on two of my feet in the process, the louts, but because of who they were, I let it slide.

We all peered through the bush. Down below was a kind of grotto. Is that a word, grotto? A ghetto? A motto? It really burns me up when I can't think of . . .

Down below was an outcropping of limestone, shall we say, that formed a ledge, a kind of shallow cave-like what-you-may-call-it on the south bank of Northup Creek. Little Alfred sat huddled at the back of the ghetto-grotto-motto, hugging his elbows for warmth and crying for his mommy.

His hair was wet and plastered all over his head, and he looked as though he could sure use a friend.

A couple of feet below the ledge sat Sinister the Bobcat, staring at the boy just the way Pete the Barncat might watch a mouse.

It's kind of spooky, the way those cats sit there without moving a hair, staring and staring and staring with their big cat eyes, and you never know what's going through their minds because they show no feeling or emotion. You know what they're going to do, but you never know whether it will be fast or slow.

Have I mentioned that I don't like cats? I don't like cats, and that goes for the big mean ones just as much as for the rinky-dink variety we have around headquarters.

From somewhere to the left, up in a tree it seemed, came a voice. "B-but P-pa, he's just a l-little b-b-b-boy!"

"Son, when you grow up, if you ever do, you'll find that this is a hard old tough world out here, and we take whatever we can git and don't ask no questions."

"Y-yeah, b-but . . ."

"You cain't serve two masters, Junior, no you cain't. You're either workin' for your stomach or you ain't workin' at all, so just hush up."

It was Wallace and Junior, as you might have already figgered out, and as usual they had arrived on the scene to serve as omens of misfortune. Sinister the Bobcat heard them arguing and gave them a cunning smile.

"Go on, Kitty," said Wallace, leaning out on his branch. "Me and my boy here don't approve of what you're fixing to do, no we don't, but still and yet . . ."

He must have leaned too far out. He lost his balance and went crashing out of the tree. When he hit the ground, Sinister wheeled around and attacked him!

"Hyah, git away from me, you dadgum cat. Junior, you git yourself down here, son, this cat ain't fooling, he's fixing to . . . !"

Fellers, that cat was something to see! Even as big as he was, he could move as quick as a . . . well, as quick as a cat, you might say. He was a very efficient killing machine, and old man Wallace was lucky that he didn't become an omen of misfortune at his own funeral.

He went squawking and flapping in a circle,

while Sinister threw up dirt with his paws and closed the gap between them.

Up in the tree, Junior hopped up and down and covered his eyes with his wings. "H-h-help, m-m-murder!"

At the last second, Wallace jumped into the air and caught an updraft and started flapping for altitude. Sinister coiled his legs under him and made a tremendous leap, snapped his jaws and came down with a mouthful of buzzard feathers.

Wallace made it back to his perch. "I ought to go back down there and thrash you good, you smart-alecky cat, you're just lucky, Junior, it's shameful the way you neglect your poor old daddy who's worked and slaved and scrimped and saved, that frazzling cat could have ate me alive, I never seen such an ungrateful, I ought to have throwed up on that cat, you just come back over here, Kitty, and I'll show you how much damage a buzzard can do!"

Sinister glared up at the buzzards, flicked his ears, and spit out the feathers. Then he turned back to the ledge, blinked his big cruel cat eyes one time, hunched down into a crouch, and began stalking Little Alfred.

It was time for action. I turned to my cannibal pals. "Guys, there's your cat. If you think you can handle . . ."

They did, because they gave a whoop and ran right over the top of me; didn't say, "Out of the way, dog" or "Excuse us please" or nothing, just by George knocked me down, plowed me under, and walked all over my face.

And the wreck was on, holy smokes, you should have seen it!

Old Sinister had pretty muchly decided that he was hot stuff, don't you see, he being your typical sneering, arrogant, self-centered, self-important cat, only four times as bad because he was four times as big.

Yes sir, he was pretty good at killing chickens and beating up buzzards and terrorizing pitiful little children, but let me tell you, fellers, he'd never seen the kind of tough that was heading his direction.

Rip and Snort just happened to be the best wrecking crew on the ranch, and Sinister knew it the minute he saw them coming. He sprang up into the air, pinned his ears back, hissed, made teeth at them, and said, "REEEEEEERRR!"

And then he sold out.

I stood up and cheered them on:

Kick him on the knee!
Slug him in the gut!
Punch him in the nose, boys.
And kick him in the . . . on the other knee!

Sinister tore a hole through that forest and ran for his life. Rip and Snort tore an even bigger hole through the forest, and the last we saw of my coyote pals, they were about to shorten that bobcat's tail another two or three inches.

I turned to Madame Moonshine. "Madame, you pulled it off. You're wonderful."

"Oh bosh! I almost ruined it all by saying bat instead of cat. You were wonderful, Hank, not me."

"Me, wonderful? Nah, it was you, Madame."

She raised a wing and primped at the feathers on her head. "Oh well, let's not argue. If you insist that I'm a wonderful witchy little owl," she turned to me with a smile, "then so be it."

Just then, I heard Little Alfred call my name.

"Madame," I said, "come on over to the ledge with me and let me introduce you to my pal Alfred."

"No, I must be going. I left Timothy alone in my cave."

"Who's Timothy?"

"Timothy, my companion and bodyguard. He's a rattlesnake. Surely you haven't forgotten Timothy."

"Oh yeah, Big Tim, the diamondback. Boy, do I remember him!"

"I left him unattended, and he has a very bad habit of getting into mischief. So . . . *adieu*."

I looked up at the gloomy sky. "No, I'd call it a rain."

I noticed that she rolled her eyes. "No, no, no! Not a dew. *Adieu*."

"Oh."

"Which means good-bye."

"Oh."

"So without further *adieu,* good-bye."

"Good-bye, Madame. Thanks for all you did, and I hope to see you somewhere down the road."

"You will, I know you will."

She hopped several times, then spread her wings and flew away into the forest.

The rain was coming down hard now, and I headed for the cave to see my little pal.

CHAPTER ELEVEN

Notch Up Another One for Hank

I sprinted across the clearing, jumped across the creek, and dived under the limestone ledge.

Seeing the expression on Little Alfred's face gave me all the reward I needed for performing amazing feats of amazing things—with a little help from Madame Moonshine, of course. I mean, the boy was just tickled to death to see me.

When I reached the ledge I was dripping wet, but that didn't seem to bother him. He came running over to me, throwed his arms around my neck, and liked to have strangled me with love.

"Hankie, you came back! I'm so gwad!"

"Well, of course I came back. Did you think I was going to leave you to the buzzards and the bobcats?"

He released me and stepped back. His eyes had grown as big as plates. "Did you see that big old tigoo?"

"It was a bob . . . no, maybe it was a tiger. Yes, I'm sure it was, probably the biggest tiger ever seen in Ochiltree County."

"The big old tigoo was going to *eat me,* but then two wolfs came and wan him away!"

"Yeah, well, I hope you understand who brought the wolves, son. They were pals of mine and I asked them to do a little favor for me, see, and, well, you know the rest of the story. I hope you'll remember this the next time your ma starts chunking rocks at me."

The smile on his face faded. His lower lip began to tremble and a tear slipped out of the corner of his eye. "I want to go home. I miss my mommy."

I lifted my head to a stern angle and gave him a severe looking-over. "I thought she was mean. I thought you were going to run away from home. I thought you didn't like your new baby sister. What's the deal?"

"I don't wike tigoos and I'm cold and I'm hungwee and I want my mommy!"

"All wight . . . all right, that is, don't cwy anymore, cry anymore. I'll take you home as soon as this rain lets up, but you've got to promise to quit pulling my tail and being a little brat. Can you do that?" He nodded. "All right, raise your right hand and repeat the Pledge: I promise to quit being a little brat."

"I pwomise to quit being a wittle bwat."

"Forever and ever and always."

"Forevoh and evoh and always."

"So help me . . ."

Suddenly I heard a fluttering noise behind me. Thinking that we were about to be attacked by Sinister the Bobcat or by my cannibal friends, I bristled, bared my fangs, whirled around, and cut loose with a deep ferocious bark.

Oh. Buzzards. Two of them. Wallace and Junior.

"Hi there, neighbor," said Wallace, "it's kindly damp out there on the limb, don't reckon y'all would mind sharing this nice dry cave with—move over, Junior, you're a-crowdin' me, son—and if y'all don't mind, we'll just sit in here 'til this shower passes over, is what we had in mind."

I swaggered over to the old man. "Are you the same guy who was up in that tree, waiting for my little pal to get attacked by a bobcat?"

His beak dropped open. "No sir, I did not, in

fact I said to Junior, and these here are my very words, I said, 'Junior, you git yourself down there and help that boy!'"

"I heard what you said, buzzard, and it would serve you right if I throwed you out into the rain."

"Now, I never, you must have misunderstood; Junior, are you gonna just sit there and let this dog . . ."

"Y-y-yeah, c-cause you d-d-did s-say that and I h-h-heard you."

Wallace glared at him. "Tattletale!"

"I m-may b-be a t-t-t-t-t-tattletale, but y-you t-t-told a b-b-big fat l-l-l-lie, big fat lie."

"That's exactly right, buzzard," I said. "You told a big fat lie."

Wallace's eyes darted back and forth between me and Junior. "Well, what did you expect? It's hard to be a Christian and a buzzard at the same time."

"That's no excuse, and unless you agree to take some punishment for being such a creep, you can just stand outside in the rain."

Wallace narrowed his eyes to slits. "I ain't ever took NO punishment from NO dog, and I ain't fixin' to start now, and I'll go stand by myself in the rain and I'll enjoy ever' minute of it because I'd rather be around ME than be around a bunch of ninnies! So there!"

And with that, he waddled out on the ledge and stood in the pouring rain. Junior turned to me and gave me a shy smile.

"H-hi, D-d-doggie. P-pa t-t-told a l-lie and y-you d-d-did r-right to m-m-make him l-l-leave."

Just then, Wallace stuck his face back inside the cave and said, "And furthermore, I hope all y'all's babies are born naked!" Then he went back out.

"Junior," I said, "I'd like for you to meet a friend of mine. This here's Little Alfred. Alfred, this here's Junior the Buzzard."

Little Alfred stared at us in amazement. "A weel buzzood?"

"That's right, son. In a year or two, you won't be able to talk back and forth with us like this, but you can now and we might as well give you the full treatment. When you get home, you can tell your ma that you met a real genuine buzzard."

"H-hi, A-a-a-a-alfred."

The boy couldn't speak. He just stared at us with shining eyes and a big smile. Just then Wallace yelled at us again.

"It's great out here, I love it, never enjoyed a rain more in my life!"

Junior grinned. "W-w-what was the p-p-pun- ishment g-g-gonna b-be?"

"Well, I was going to make your old man join us in singing a nice happy song about all the won- derful things we enjoy about this life. He's such a grouch, I figgered that would hurt him as bad as anything."

"Y-y-y-yeah, h-he'd h-hate that!"

I went to the edge of the cave. Old Wallace was out there all humped over and dripping water and grumbling to himself.

"How's the weather out there, Wallace?"

"Wonderful! I still love it!"

"You sure you don't want to come back inside and take your punishment?"

"Puppy, I ain't never took no . . ."

At that very moment a bolt of lightning came crashing down and struck a big cottonwood tree right in front of us. Leaves and tree bark went flying in all directions and there was a terrible *BOOM!*

Wallace squawked and jumped so high that he landed back inside the cave. "On second thought, a little punishment is good for the soul. What is it you have in mind, dog?"

"We're all going to sing a little song."

"I hate songs!"

"About the things we love most in this life."

"I hate love!"

"And you're going to do a verse, the same as the rest of us."

"I hate music and I can't sing!"

"Then get back out there in the rain."

"On the other hand, a guy can always try."

"That's better."

"But that don't mean I'll like it."

"That's fine, you don't have to like it."

"Good, because I won't."

I went through the song and showed them how it was done. Then I did the first verse, and when I finished we went around the circle and each of us did a verse. Even Little Alfred did one. The song was called "I Love All Kinds of Stuff," and here's how it went.

Hank:
I love the septic tank's
Emerald waters bank to bank,
Oh, I love the septic tank,
It makes my life worthwhile.

Junior:
I love pretty girls,
They make my feathers want to curl,

Oh! I love pretty girls,
They make my life worthwhile.

Alfred:
I wuv pwaying twucks,
I wuv my mommy vewy much,
I wuv her tender touch,
It makes my wife worffwhile.

Well, it was Wallace's turn. We all looked at him and waited for him to come up with a verse. He had his wings folded across his chest and a huge scowl on his face.

"Your turn, Wallace, jump right in there."

"What's a 'twuck'? I never heard of a twuck; and Junior, you wouldn't know what to do with a pretty girl if you found one!"

"Y-y-yeah, b-but I c-could t-t-t-try."

"And anybody that was dumb enough to spend time in a septic tank . . ."

"Sing, buzzard, or go stand in the rain!"

"All right, I'll sing, but I ain't gonna like it and it ain't gonna be pretty! 'I love . . . I love . . . I love . . .' What key's it in, I cain't find the note!"

"It won't matter, Wallace, just grab a note and run with it."

"All right, you asked for it!"

Wallace:
I love being mad,
Yelling, scolding, talking bad,
I love being called a cad,
It makes my life worthwhile.

After we'd each done our verses, we put them all together and sang them in harmony. Boy, did we cut loose and sing! It must have been pretty good, because when we were done the rain had stopped and the sun had broken through the clouds.

I turned to Wallace. "Now, wasn't that fun? Go ahead and admit it, we won't tell anybody."

"No, it wasn't no fun at all. I hate music, I hate singing, I hate love, and I hate fun."

"Wallace, you're nothing but a cad."

His face burst into a smile. "Now you're talkin', dog, I love that!"

The old fool, I pushed him off the ledge and he flew away. Then I turned to Junior. "Well, the rain's quit and I've got to get this boy back to his ma. See you again sometime. It was fun."

"Y-y-yeah, it s-s-sure w-w-was. I l-love to s-s-sing."

Little Alfred hadn't said a word. He was hanging back kind of bashful-like and had a finger in his mouth. "Good-bye, Junyo. I wike buzzoods."

"B-b-bye, L-little A-alfred."

And with that, Junior jumped off the ledge and flapped his big wings and flew away.

I took a deep breath and turned to Alfred.

"Well, son, you've had a rare opportunity to meet some of my friends. One of these days, when you're all growed up, you'll look back at this day and wonder if it really happened. And it did."

He nodded and smiled, and the sparkle in his eyes was prettier than any star I'd ever seen.

"Now let's see if we can sneak you back home without getting both of us in a world of trouble."

And with that, we left our adventures behind us and headed for the house.

CHAPTER TWELVE

A Hero Again, What More Can I Say?

You might be wondering how I found my way out of the Dark Unchanted Forest, after I'd spent so much of the afternoon lost in it.

Simple, and you might want to remember this. I just followed Northup Creek in a northerly direction until it joined Wolf Creek, because I knew that it would, and once we made it to Wolf Creek we were out of the woods, so to speak, and I knew the way home from there.

Pretty slick, huh? You bet it was.

We waded across Wolf Creek, made our way through the willows in the creek bed, climbed up the sandy bank, and started walking the last quarter-mile to the house.

It was a triumphant procession and I could

114

almost hear the marching music in the background. I was out front in the lead, which was only right since I had . . . well, we needn't dwell on the obvious . . . but I was out there in front of the procession, while Little Alfred brought up the rear.

I told the boy to pick up his feet and stay in step. I knew we'd draw a crowd, see, and that every eye would be on the returning heroes, and I wanted our little outfit to look snappy and make a deep and lasting impression on the multitude.

Very few details escape my attention, and I noticed right away that Drover, my second in command, didn't sound the alarm or come rushing out to bark at us as we approached the house.

The reason he didn't was that he was playing Chase and Romp with Pete the Barncat, which sort of burned me up and introduced the only sour note into what was otherwise a near-perfect ending to an exciting day.

It's terrible to be so involved in your work, so devoted to your job that you can't even enjoy a parade without finding flaws and noticing that it ain't perfect. But that's part of the price we pay for being in the security business.

Drover didn't pick us up until we were about a hundred feet south of the gas tanks, and then it was the cat who saw us first.

"My goodness, look what's coming our way! It's Hankie the Wonder Dog and the missing child."

"Oh my gosh, Hank's gonna be . . . I forgot all about . . . I never should have let you . . ."

He came ripping down the hill, giving off his usual "yip-yip-yip," which wouldn't scare a flea, but at least he was making a showing.

"Oh gosh, you're back, Hank, I'm so glad! And I guess you found Little Alfred."

"Looks that way, don't it?"

"Did you run into that bobcat?"

"It was a full-grown tiger, must have weighed five to six hundred pounds."

"A tiger?"

"That's correct. Yes, I found the full-grown tiger. Yes, he was stalking Little Alfred. Yes, I gave him a thrashing he won't soon forget. And yes, you missed all the adventure."

"Yeah, but I didn't miss it by much. If this old leg . . ."

"Forget the leg, Drover."

"What leg?"

"Your so-called bad leg."

"Oh, that one. Heck, I'd just about forgotten about it."

"Good. Let's leave it at that. Where is everyone?"

"Well, let's see." He sat down and scratched on his ear. "I'm here and Pete's over there in the yard. J. T. Cluck's up by the machine shed and . . ."

"Loper and Sally May, you weed!"

"Oh. Gee, maybe they're out looking for Little Alfred, you reckon?"

"That sounds plausible. They're out looking for the lost child and you're here at the house, playing footsie with the cat."

"It was Chase and Romp, and Pete made me play. He said . . ."

"Never mind what he said. Your conduct was disgraceful and I'll have to put this in my report."

"Oh drat."

"And now, if you'll stand back I will sound the alarm and alert Little Alfred's parents that he is safe."

I switched my Barking Alert Mode over to manual and went through the All's Clear, All's Well procedure. Within a matter of minutes, Loper rode his horse out of the creek bottom and Sally May popped out of the willows.

She was carrying Little Molly, the poor child with the lizard face, in a blanket, and she approached us in a rapid walk. Sally May did, not Molly. She was a baby. Sally May wasn't a baby, Molly was, and she approached us . . . oh forget it.

I had seen that walk before and it made me a little nervous to see it again.

See, when Sally May gets into that foxtrot, she's usually mad and armed with rocks. I considered racing away from the scene but decided to stand my ground and risk a bombardment.

As she approached, I could see that her hair was wet and stringy, and that anger had left its tracks upon her brow, so to speak. Both were bad signs.

"Alfred, where on earth have you been? We've been worried sick about you, we thought you were lost. Oh Alfred, why do you do things like this to your parents?"

Alfred hung his head. I did the same, and also thumped my tail on the ground. Alfred didn't thump his tail because . . . well, of course he didn't, because he didn't have one.

"I'm sowwy, Mom. I wan away fwom home, but I got wost in the woods and I didn't wike it and I'm never going to wun away again."

After Sally May's glare had scorched the boy, she turned it on me. "Did YOU lead my boy into the pasture?"

HUH? Me? Now wait a minute!

"Hank, you scoundrel, I don't know what I'm going to do with you!" Her eyes went back to

119

Alfred. "Or you." Back to me. "You're both incorrigible!" Back to Alfred. "Honey, why did you want to run away from home?"

Alfred was about to cry again. "Well, you bwought home that baby and you didn't want me anymore!"

"Oh Alfred, how could you even think such a thing?" She knelt down and gathered him up in her arms. "Mommy loves you very, very much, but for a while she's going to be busy with your new sister. I'll tell you what. If you'll help me take care of Molly, we can be together and we'll both feel better about it. How does that sound?"

She hugged him hard and ran her fingers through his wet hair. Then her glare hit me again. "And don't you ever, EVER go off in the pasture with that dog again!"

The boy pulled away from her arms. "But Mom, I went awone and Hank saved me!"

"Ummmm." I could tell she didn't believe him.

"He bwought two wolfs that came and saved me fwom a big huge tigoo!"

"Two wolves? A tiger!"

I, uh, took this opportunity to, uh, study the clouds. The, uh, animals in question were coyotes rather than wolves, and the, uh, villain in the case had been . . . well, maybe *bobcat* would have

120

been more accurate, but he was definitely as big as any tiger I'd ever run into. Don't you see.

Alfred went on with his story. "And the wolfs beat up the tigoo and then Hank came and wicked my face and I met a weal buzzood!"

Sally May flinched on that word. "A buzzard!"

"And I talked to him and he talked to me!"

Loper had ridden up by this time and had stepped out of the saddle. Sally May gave him a long questioning look. "Do you hear what your son is saying?"

"Yup. Two wolves ran off a tiger and he met a buzzard, and Hank did something or other. Sounds like a windy tale to me."

Alfred's little mouth drew up into a pout. "It's not a windy tale, it's twue! Hank is my fwiend and I want him to sweep in my bed wiff me tonight."

There was a long silence. Loper shifted his weight from one leg to the other. His horse swished his tail at a fly. Sally May rocked Molly back and forth in her arms and studied Loper's face. After a bit, he gave his head the slightest of nods.

Sally May turned back to Alfred. "All right, just this once we'll let Hank sleep in your room, but only if you promise never to run away again."

Little Alfred gave a cheer and went flying around in circles. I was about to join him when Sally May caught me by a front leg and pulled me back. She spoke to me in a low, severe tone of voice.

"Now listen to me, you oaf, I don't know what really went on this afternoon, but I know that you were involved in it up to your ears." I whapped my tail. "Against my better judgment, I'm going to let you sleep with my child because, for reasons that I don't understand, he seems fond of you."

I whapped my tail. She leveled a finger at my nose. "But if you throw up on my clean floor or wet on my nice furniture or dig holes in my sheets, Hank, I swear I'll . . ." She closed her eyes and shook her head and smiled and stood up. "They're impossible, both of them. One's just as bad as the other."

"Shall I do the honors?" Loper asked.

"Please, and thank you."

"Come on, Hank, let's put this horse up and then we'll get to the fun part."

I turned to Drover. "You see what comes of being a chickenhearted little mutt? I'm going to be decorated for heroism in the line of duty, while you stay outside with your friend the cat.

No risk, no reward, Drover, and with that I bid you good night."

"Good night, Hank, I'll miss you."

"You bet you will."

I marched down to the corral beside my master and stood guard at the saddle shed while he put up his rigging. My head was filled with visions of what was to come: a banquet in my honor; a toast to the Head of Ranch Security; speeches, applause, adoring gazes; a nice juicy steak bone . . .

What a lousy trick!

The so-called "honors" turned out to be a trip to the bathtub. I was throwed into a tub of scalding hot water, scrubbed with stinking soap and a hard-bristle brush, de-ticked, de-flead, de-dirted, de-scented, almost de-skinned, and derned near drownded.

When I crawled out of that dipping vat, fellers, I could hardly stand myself.

But cleanliness hath a few rewards. I was allowed to camp out with Little Alfred, even slept in the bed with him, which was the first time that miracle had ever happened. And I'm proud to report that I maintained control of all my various bodily processes and fluids, so to speak, and didn't make a single mess. Not one!

I know you think I'm lying, but . . . oh, there was one small mishap in the middle of the night, but it occurred under the bed and Sally May didn't find it until weeks later. By that time I was well out of her range.

Around here, the endings don't come any happier than that.

Case closed.

Have you read all of Hank's adventures?

□ Yes I want to join Hank's Security Force. Enclosed is $11.95 ($8.95 + $3.00 for shipping and handling) for my **two-year membership**. [Make check payable to Maverick Books.]

Which book would you like to receive in your Welcome Package? Choose from books 1–30.

(#   )   (#   )

FIRST CHOICE   SECOND CHOICE

                                          BOY or GIRL

YOUR NAME   (CIRCLE ONE)

MAILING ADDRESS

CITY   STATE   ZIP

TELEPHONE   BIRTH DATE

E-MAIL

Are you a □ Teacher or □ Librarian?

Send check or money order for $11.95 to:

Hank's Security Force
Maverick Books
PO Box 549
Perryton, Texas 79070

DO NOT SEND CASH. NO CREDIT CARDS ACCEPTED.
Allow 4–6 weeks for delivery.

The Hank the Cowdog Security Force, the Welcome Package, and The Hank Times are the sole responsibility of Maverick Books. They are not organized, sponsored, or endorsed by Penguin Putnam Inc., Puffin Books, Viking Children's Books, or their subsidiaries or affiliates.